S,

GINA BRIGANTI

Saunders' Choice
A Natural Gifts Novella
By Gina Briganti
Copyright 2020
Cover design by Victoria Cooper Art

ISBN: Print 978-1-7338028-2-6
ISBN: Ebook 978-1-7338028-3-3

Dedication

This book is dedicated to my granddaughter, Lilli.

Thank You

Thank you to Antonina Lackey, Carolyn Rae, and Kris Jayne for sharing your valued opinions as I was writing Saunders' Choice. I appreciate you more than words can say!

Also by Gina Briganti

<u>Natural Gifts Series</u>
The Dreaming (Book 1)
Desert Sunrise (Book 2)
No Yesterdays (Book 3)
Deep In The Dreaming (Book 4)

<u>Non-Fiction</u>
Keep It Simple: Permission to Illuminate Your Life Easily, Effortlessly, & Joyfully
The Reiki Café: Reiki III (ART) Manual

Chapter 1

Laughter followed Velvet as she left the stage in the grotto where she had been hired to perform a private show for the wealthy creatures's birthday party.

She knew the crowd were eyeing her bare torso, hoping the current would sway her long silver and lilac-tinted hair off of her breasts so they could see if the color of her nipples matched the color of her lilac fin.

She sighed. Maybe it was time to change. Raven black hair with a bright, shiny aqua blue tail made her audiences stare, but she did get more jobs that way. She wanted more shows at the big clubs.

"Velvet." Cassidy, her manager, called out to her from where she waited in the luxurious apartment the management called a dressing room.

Cassidy was a mermaid, too. She was much older than Velvet, who was only one hundred years old. Cassidy was more than three hundred years old. No one would know that if it weren't for the Hall of Records there in The Dreaming because everything stayed the way you wanted it to.

Cassidy looked exactly the way she wanted to look. As did Velvet. As did the club she performed in. It was the perfection of everything in her life that had developed Velvet's sense of humor to begin with. She needed a break from the sameness of perfection.

"Cassidy," she sang back in answer, turning her bubbles into kissing lips that smacked Cassidy on the cheek when they reached her. They made a smacking sound for the kiss, and then popped, returning to the water.

"They liked you." Cassidy leaned back in the purple chair, releasing smoky tendrils from her lungs and her cigarette while she spoke.

Velvet had to smile at Cassidy's mimicry of 1950's television where the characters were in black and white, with cigarette in hand, and an evening cocktail on the table in front of them. She had styled her hair, and colored it, to match Lucy Ricardo's ravishing red in the *I love Lucy* show. Her tail matched. She was more modest than Velvet, too, because she wore black shells to cover her breasts.

"They did like me," Velvet agreed. "My new set about the dangers of washing and styling your hair in a whirlpool went over well with the females."

Velvet treated Cassidy to the joke that received the most laughs; "So the big night is finally here. You know the one I mean, ladies," Velvet comically winked at Cassidy, "all the signs are there." Velvet theatrically swung her left arm in front of her, pointing the index finger up. "One, he brought you over to his mother's house for dinner. Two," Velvet swung her arm around and brought her middle finger up to join the index finger, "he used the word *future* in a sentence." Velvet paused for those crucial seconds to let Cassidy laugh and then started the next part of the joke. "And three, he said he's taking you somewhere special. You have to look amazing. There will be pictures and you will be telling the story for years about how you knew this was the night. So, what do you do, ladies?" Velvet paused for one second. "You decide to try the new trend." Her voice turned mocking. "On the most important night of your life, you mess with what he likes about you."

Cassidy laughed, then sipped from her bourbon, leaning forward to listen to the rest of the joke.

"Yes, you mess with what's working." Velvet bumped the microphone in her right hand against her head. "I know, I know. You saw it in a magazine. It looked so glamorous. A wild new you. You messed with what was working. You put your head in a whirlpool and let it style your hair for you. Wait, wait, that's not even the topper. You asked someone to show you where the best whirlpool is." Velvet shook her head, laughing along with Cassidy, and the memory of the crowd's raucous laughter during the show. "Really, does it matter how good your hair looks if you're late and can't swim right for a week from the force of the whirlpool?" Velvet paused, then laughed at herself. "Who am I kidding? Of course it's worth it."

Cassidy fell over laughing, barely holding onto her drink.

Velvet loved to see people laugh and smile. Both were common enough in The Dreaming. Still, it was a thrill to know that she was the one causing the laughter and smiles. Especially when they were genuine. She could fill the audience with her own creations; a dream audience who looked and acted the way she directed them to. The real thing was so much more satisfying. Her sister Noelia was content with dream creations for her audience of readers. Velvet envied Noelia the pleasure she saw on her face when she released a new book and her creations clamored for it.

Secretly, Velvet had tried to create a packed stadium full of adoring fans who stroked every one of her ego's urges. She had felt worse than when she started doing stand up and she was genuinely booed for her boring jokes and nervous delivery. Genuine emotion was definitely her style.

"That's my favorite," Cassidy said.

Cassidy said that about all of Velvet's new jokes. She also meant it about each joke.

"Thanks." Velvet bowed. "So, what is the champagne for?" Velvet read the label and raised an eyebrow, waiting for an answer.

Cassidy clapped her hands, giddy with excitement. "You have been offered a tour! With Rockford Entertainment. You'll be travelling with other headliners. They showed me the PR campaign, and it is gorgeous. You'll be performing in front of full audiences every night. The best part is, they called me, not the other way around. They want you, kid."

"They want me with the lilac tail?" Velvet asked doubtfully.

"Where has your confidence gone? Of course they want you with the lilac tail. You're a comedian, not a model. What is this about? This tour is exactly what you've been working for."

Cassidy's concern was real. Velvet was never down. Her sunny personality was one of the main reasons she accepted her as a client. She had enough nervous Nellies and dour Dominicks.

Velvet let out a deep sigh, and then leaned back in her chair. "I think I've been putting too much pressure on myself. I'm writing good stuff and working steadily. There's no reason for me to feel like my career isn't going the way I want it to."

"I know what this is about," Cassidy said in her wisest voice. "This is about Ronolo and Delia getting together and manifesting a baby so soon after your breakup with him. You broke up with him, remember? He wanted you to settle down, forget about your career, and raise babies. If he was the one for you, you would have wanted the same things he did."

"I know all of that, Cassidy. He's a great male, and I do miss him sometimes. I should get out and mingle more. Of course, that's going to be easy because I will be on the road!" The excitement of the tour caught up to Velvet, chasing her doubts away.

Chapter 2

Velvet enjoyed the manifestation created by her roommate. The rooms they were given by management on this tour were meant for one small creature. Debra immediately gave them bigger bedrooms, separate bathrooms, closets, and dressing tables in each hotel they stayed in.

Velvet couldn't say for sure what Debra was, as species go, and she didn't know her well enough to ask. Debra looked human with her blue eyes, black hair, and perfectly shaped body, but few of her actions were human. She used advanced magic much more freely than humans allowed themselves to in the Dreaming. She had no trouble that Velvet could see with creating anything she wanted to.

Humans didn't come to live in the Dreaming, anyway. They were called visitors because they stayed for short periods of time. Her friend Joe was the only human she knew who visited the Dreaming every time he fell asleep.

Debra's comedy routine on this tour was about how being a professional comedian makes relationships difficult. Debra's jokes about how partners swung back and forth between wanting her to be funny and wanting her to be normal made her and the audiences laugh.

Velvet laughed as she remembered Debra's outraged impression of a boyfriend during a fight because she told him a joke and he laughed, breaking the mood of the fight. "Now, I ask you," Debra played to the audience, "next to sex, isn't laughter the best way to stop a fight?" Debra always took a drink from her ginger ale to let the audience think before she delivered the punch line; "He started the next fight. Do you know what we fought about? We fought about me ending the last fight with a joke."

Velvet and Debra were placed together in each hotel, since female comedians were rare, even in the Dreaming. Velvet had spent enough time researching them in the Hall of Records, watching videos there, to know that female comedians were rare in the World, too.

The tour was halfway over now. They all had the afternoon off to do whatever they wanted. Velvet was going swimming.

Most of the tour was in parts of the Dreaming that were mirror images of the World, where oceans filled with mermaids weren't everyday scenery.

She was wearing legs instead of fins on stage. Her gills were covered by her long hair. She looked more human than she was comfortable with; being a mermaid was what she wanted. She shrugged. She loved the big crowds they were playing to.

Exploring a new ocean sounded good to her today. Pushing through the water, letting it force her hair to float behind her, was ecstasy for Velvet.

Brightly colored fish swam past her. There were unfamiliar dolphins, whales, octopi, and creatures in every direction. It did pay to travel to the dry land parts of the Dreaming if it led to new waterways to explore.

"Hello." Velvet greeted a young dolphin who was playing close to an older dolphin. Velvet made sure that the older dolphin could see and hear what she said to the youngster.

"Hello," he answered back in a friendly voice.

"I'm Velvet. I'm visiting here for a couple of days. This is my first visit to this part of the Dreaming. I don't know anyone here."

The older dolphin swam close to Velvet, looking her over. "I'm Shadow."

Velvet felt that she had passed a test. "I'm happy to meet you, Shadow."

Shadow was a bottlenose dolphin, grey in color. She and the younger creature were almost too much like their counterparts in the World, except that they were here. They obviously belonged here because of their animated faces and their ability to speak.

"I'm Tubbins," the younger dolphin told her, smiling and playing with a bright blue fish.

"This is a beautiful ocean," Velvet said. *Will I ever see all of the Dreaming*?

"We like living here. Where are you visiting from?" Asked Shadow.

Addresses didn't work the same way in the Dreaming as they did in what Velvet knew of the World. Instead of describing a city and a state, Velvet created a visual to show to Shadow of the sandcastle she liked to stay in with her friend, Riddle. It was his construction, but it suited her so well it could be her own.

"That's a lovely sandcastle. I see it's under a lake? How interesting. Do you like living in the lake?" Asked Shadow.

"Mostly I like living near my friends and family. The lake is where they choose to be, and I choose to be with them. I sometimes go exploring, like I am now, to see new places."

"I should take Tubbins to visit a lake. Thank you for the idea," Shadow said as she turned to Tubbins. "Tubbins, it's time for lunch. Tell Manny that we'll see him later when he comes over this evening." Shadow turned back to Velvet, saying, "Those two can play all day and all night. They never get tired, and they don't fight much. It's nice meeting you, Velvet. I hope to see you again."

Velvet blew Shadow a kiss, and then tossed a toy ship she manifested for Tubbins to him as she waved goodbye.

Swimming along, Velvet continued to send a friendly wave to every creature she saw. She rounded the corner of a huge coral reef and saw a murky, shaded part of the coral ahead. If she had a middle name, it would be Curious. Velvet thought nothing of swimming into the darkened water.

A naked man was swimming furiously to the surface, struggling and thrashing in a panic.

He thinks he's drowning.

If his panic didn't give him away as a visitor to the Dreaming, his energy did. She didn't know many visitors, but she had met more than anyone else she knew. Why did she find visitors so compelling? She often wondered about that.

Once, she had shared a romance with a visitor. His name was Joe, and he was sixteen years old at the time. For one whole summer, that was what he called it, they spent all of his time in the Dreaming together. Then Joe admitted to her that he felt weird about having an invisible girlfriend, and they stopped seeing one another in that way. They were friends now. He'd long since grown up and was happily married to a new visitor to the Dreaming. A woman named Dana.

Velvet stopped her reverie and flashed into action, quickly pushing the stranger to what would appear to be a surface to him. She held him while he gulped air, and spurted water from his mouth at the same time.

The stranger turned wild eyes to Velvet. He scanned her from head to tail, and then started racing away from her.

"What?" Velvet called out sarcastically. "Was it something I said? Most people have to know me awhile before they swim away at high speed." As soon as she said it, she felt terrible and her compassion kicked her butt. She called out, "I'm sorry. I hope you're okay."

The visitor never looked back.

Chapter 3

Debra, Velvet, and the rest of the comedians took their final bows and made their way to the lobby. Two more stops and the tour would be over. No one was happy with the club they were in right now. It smelled like a locker room. The drinks looked, smelled, and tasted wrong. The audience...well, there would not be any shaking hands with the crowd tonight.

Debra launched herself at Domino, the tour manager, as soon as he couldn't hide from them anymore. "Did you lose a bet, or did you lose your mind?"

"Listen, the guy who owns this place is a friend of the guy who owns The Sky Rocket. We had to play here in order to play there. You do want to play The Sky Rocket, don't you?"

He had them there.

"How about a little warning, then?" Velvet suggested. "Like now, we have one night at The Sky Rocket and one night at Shugey's. What's Shugey's like, Domino?"

Domino moved a few steps away before he answered. He mumbled, "Better than here. That's good, right?"

Domino liked to dress in black and white, which is where he earned his nickname. He was one of the rare creatures in the Dreaming who liked to change his form, but keep his clothes the same each time he dressed. Today, he looked like a cross between a gorilla and a giraffe. It was bizarre, to say the least.

Debra was not letting him off easy. "Listen, Domino, I didn't come on this tour to play places like this. I started in better dumps where I played for a drink and a snack. I wouldn't dare to drink what they hand out here. Did you see the color of their *water*?"

"So change it-" Domino started to say, but then Mikey, who looked like a gorilla all the time, started growling and chasing after him. Mikey's act was strictly physical comedy. Velvet would not have guessed that he could be as scary as he was right now.

"He ate something that was in a bowl on the table in the back," Debra explained to the rest of them.

"Poor guy. Do you think he's going to be okay?" Velvet murmured, watching him for signs that he wasn't. Since he had the energy to pursue Domino, he was probably okay.

"So, two more stops, and then I know better than to book with this guy again." Velvet shrugged and left it at that.

"I have more to say than that," Paulo of the Latin lover comedy act announced as he pointed out the yellow goo sticking to his shoes. "Did you get it on you, too?"

Paulo inspected our shoes and learned that he had collected it all himself. "Fantastico." He groaned, and then threw the ruined shoes in the trash.

Mikey rejoined them, alone, grunting with satisfaction. "We don't have to play Shugey's unless we want to. Do we want to?" His voice was deep and gruff. It fit him.

"I vote no," Debra sniffed, and then laid her hand on Mikey's arm. "Thank you for squaring that, Mikey. You're a heck of a gorilla."

Velvet thought she saw a blush darken Mikey's cheeks.

"I'll pass, too," Velvet voted. She would rather spend the time swimming the new parts of the ocean they were near.

Paulo's phone rang, showing an incoming call from Domino. He answered on speaker. "Si, Domino. What do you want?"

"Paulo, you know Shugey's, right? Tell them it's not as bad as this place." Domino pleaded with the one talent on the tour who was trying to get his big break.

Maybe Domino was drinking too much these days.

"We're voting on it," Paulo told him. Tall, handsome, and muscular, he fit most visions of a Latin lover.

Domino sighed. He knew he wasn't getting his show at Shugey's.

"Goodnight," Velvet called out cheerfully, waving goodbye to her co-workers when she finished removing her stage makeup. "See you at The Sky Rocket, if I don't see you before that."

Knowing that she had only one more day to explore that part of the Dreaming, Velvet took advantage and swam out into another new part of the ocean. Here the water was bubbly and warm, a natural hot spring. Velvet relaxed and allowed the bubbles to massage her back and neck.

Domino surprised her by approaching her in a blended form of a water snake and a seahorse. He looked like an extra-long, coiled, seahorse. In the absence of his usual black and white clothing, he colored himself in black and white triangles.

Velvet couldn't hold her curiosity any longer. "Domino, where do you get your ideas? You always surprise me."

Domino's seahorse mouth was able to smile. "They come to me, maybe the same way your ideas come to you? Some pop into my head, already formed. Others I work with until I like what I see. The more outrageous I look, the more comfortable I feel. Creatures stare, but this way I know why."

Velvet nodded because ideas did come to her in a variety of ways. "Would you like some bubbles?" She graciously offered to move over, even though the spot she was in was prime and she was enjoying it. Domino had sought her out for a reason, and having to cancel their show at Shugey's might have been hard for him. She reasoned that he would benefit from the bubbles more than she could.

"You're too kind, Velvet. I could use a massage right now, and a friend. I'm going to lose my job over the cancellation. Mr. Headliner complained about playing the dive last night. He called his agent from the dressing room. Who knows why he went on stage?" Domino shook his head, a puzzled look on his face.

Velvet placed a gentle hand on his back, up high enough that she didn't think she could possibly be touching anything private. "Are you sure you're going to lose your job over this, Domino? I wouldn't want you to worry for no reason."

Some creatures did that all too often, in Velvet's opinion. They worried and wasted energy on things that never happened. It was almost as though they didn't remember that they lived in paradise.

They floated in silence. The way he hid his face and tried to choke back tears tore at her heart.

The comedian in Velvet had to try to cheer Domino up. She started by coloring the plants and rocks around them black and white. Then she created a pirate ship and placed performers on the deck in full pirate costume. They were dancing to *Rock Me Amadeus* by Falco.

Domino's tears disappeared, and then he started to laugh the way creatures did when they let go of their tension. Some of his coils around the middle of his form loosened.

"Velvet," he tried to say between belly laughs that bounced his coils up and down, "you are amazing. I knew you were the one to talk to."

Velvet smiled wide and bowed. "I'm happy to help." She returned to her set of bubbles and allowed them to relax her once again.

Domino lounged on the good jets for a while, and then turned to ask her another question. "Are you upset with me about that club?"

"Upset is too strong a word. I didn't like it, and it's the worst club I've played, but I was disappointed that you did that to us without a warning. So, if you like your job as much as you say you do, then I suggest you don't trick your talent into playing clubs like that one in the future."

She'd never used a biting tone with him before, but pretending she wasn't upset with him wouldn't be fair. He had to learn.

He shifted her way, to face her. "I'm sorry. It was a crummy thing to do. None of you should have been there without knowing the terms of the deal. I thought I was being clever."

Velvet saw his coils start to droop again and reached out to pat an upper coil. "Lesson learned, where I'm concerned. Why don't you try to apologize to the others and see what happens? Especially Stewie. Maybe you can still fix it."

Stewie, who Domino called Mr. Headliner, was a star. A household name. He was drawing seventy-five percent of the crowd, and all of the talent respected his instincts. Like Domino,

Velvet wondered why Stewie went on last night at all? He could have walked out.

Domino's black triangles looked gray, and the smile disappeared again.

"All you have to do is apologize. You don't have to ask him for anything. You can do this, Domino. You can."

"I can apologize. It's two words. Or six, if I add 'I made a mistake' to it. Thanks, Velvet. Say, is there anything I can do for you? It means a lot to me that you were willing to help me."

The black pigment was returning, darkening his black triangles.

"No, your apology is enough for me. I know you didn't trick us for a bad reason. You made a mistake." Her shrug was pure Velvet. Simple and honest.

Domino smiled in a way that told Velvet he was well on his way to becoming a more confident tour manager. Good for him.

"Take the good bubbles then." He scooted over, and then stretched out to an impressive length. He was as long as the pirate ship. "Are you going to leave the pirate ship here? It's funny. Divers will probably have a good time with it."

"I will, Domino. That's a good idea." The effervescence was almost too good. Velvet relaxed until no more thoughts popped into her head. Domino had said goodbye long ago, and the water was darker than before when she opened her eyes.

Velvet stretched and looked for clues about how long she had been mindless. Not all of the water was darker, she noticed. Only that one spot.

It reminded her of the one other time she saw a darker spot of water. She ventured closer, reaching out one hand to feel for a difference in the texture there.

As before, the naked man struggled to rise to the surface, glancing between her and the animated pirate ship.

"It's okay," Velvet said firmly. "Calm down. You are not drowning. You are safe."

He hesitantly stopped thrashing and stared hard at her face. "Am I dead?"

Velvet was stunned into silence. She hadn't considered the possibility. Finally, she answered honestly. "I don't know. All I know is that you're a visitor because you keep thinking you're drowning."

"I, I –" He started to fade.

She made careful notes in her memory about him. She was going to find out about the hazel-eyed, tanned, sandy-haired visitor who was inches taller than her.

In terms of the World, he was probably in his third decade of life. Maybe knowing more about him would be what she needed to find out more about him.

Chapter 4

Velvet turned from her side of The Sky Rocket's dressing table so that she was facing Debra. They were both getting ready for the party Domino was giving to thank them for not having him fired. It was also the end-of-the-tour party. If she and Debra didn't stay in touch, she wouldn't be able to ask her what type of creature she was. Maybe she still didn't know her well enough to ask the question, but she was going for it anyway.

"Debra, I've enjoyed this tour much more than I would have if you weren't here. Thanks for all the nice things you've done for me, and for everyone else."

Debra smiled and finished fluffing her hair, looking at Velvet sideways in the mirror. "Same here. You're a nice creature."

"You know what I'm wondering about, don't you?" Velvet tilted her head to the side.

"I read people well," Debra admitted. "I'm not any different than the other creatures here, besides being a lot older. You know, in the World, many females don't like to reveal their ages."

"I know. I'm interested in the World, too. Not many of the creatures I know are. Most creatures don't call our world the Dreaming, like we do. I'm more curious about you now than I was before."

Debra nodded, and Velvet could see that she asked herself a question, and that she made a decision.

"I want to impart something to you. I am twenty thousand years old." Debra said, and then was silent.

"Thank you for giving me time to adjust to hearing that. I think that makes you as old as Riddle. Older than the Dreaming."

"Yes, we are of an age. Are you surprised that I know him?" Debra leaned back on her lounging couch, looking like a glamorous Hollywood film star.

If she doesn't want to talk about where she came from. I'll stick with what she will talk about. "I'm surprised when anyone knows him. He keeps to himself. He trusts me because in the time I've known him, I haven't disappointed him."

"Riddle has reason to be cautious. Some of his experiments were-" Debra stopped herself.

Velvet put Debra at ease by finishing the sentence. "The reason why he looks the way he does now."

Riddle's head was where others usually had their knees, resting on his feet, which rested on the sandy floor of his underwater lake home. His arms came out of his head, where his ears should be, his chest rested on top of his head, and his legs were on top of his chest. His ears were located on his knees. His groin was bare and sexless.

The hardest part for Velvet was that Riddle didn't understand the concept of clothes. She supposed that because he didn't have any genitals, or nipples, it wasn't a big deal.

"Yes. I can see why you and Riddle are friends. You're a sensitive creature, especially for a sarcastic comedian."

"Ha!" Velvet laughed whole-heartedly, repaying Debra's compliment. The best compliment a comedian can receive is a genuine laugh.

"Let's go have some fun at this wrap party, eh?" Debra held her elegant arm out to Velvet's, and the two sashayed from the dressing room out to the club's dance floor to join the rest of the cast.

Domino approached them, wearing a big, truly happy, smile. He had changed his appearance in Velvet's honor to a black and white checkered merman.

"You are the creature of the hour," Domino told Velvet. "Thanks to you, I still have a job. The new contracts make it impossible for me to make a decision like the last one, and I've already landed a few great comedians for my next tour. I hope you two will join us," he said carefully.

"Thank you." Debra smiled at him, her energy and her expression making it almost impossible for Velvet to believe she was one of the oldest creatures in the Dreaming.

Domino bowed, and then floated away to talk to more new arrivals.

"Are you considering another Rockford tour?" Debra asked her before discretely pulsing some magic into her chest that plumped her lush, already impressive breasts.

A quick glance showed Velvet that Rod, the owner of The Sky Rocket, was on his way over to them.

So, she liked The Rod, did she? Velvet looked to Debra for cues on whether she wanted to talk with him on her own, or whether she wanted her to stay and be a part of the conversation.

Debra made a subtle motion to tell Velvet that she wanted her to stay with them for a little while.

Rod swayed through the room, looking and acting every inch the cocky owner of a famous night club. Velvet wouldn't mind joining Mikey when it was a good time for it. Debra must know something she didn't about Rod. Velvet had to believe that, otherwise she would give Debra an out to sit with her and Mikey.

Rod opened his conversation to Debra with what he obviously considered a joke. "Is that drink stiff enough for you?"

He ignored Velvet, which was a relief for her.

Velvet could see that Debra was in her own depth and murmured her goodbyes.

Mikey spoke in his shy voice as Velvet joined him. She knew from experience that he liked sitting with her at meals because she didn't eat, and she made him feel comfortable. She always ordered the good stuff and gave her food to him. If she ever needed a favor, he'd be there. She'd made a good friend on this tour.

After dinner Domino entertained them all by standing in the middle of the room and telling his own jokes. She liked seeing him try to do what they did. He definitely had a better idea of what it meant to stand up there now.

Next tour, he planned to open with a dinner like this one and show them that he respected what it took to stand up on stage night after night and try to get a laugh out of creatures.

He did tell a joke or two that made them genuinely laugh. "If I was a comedian, I would have it written into my contract that I only play four drink minimum clubs. Crazy eyes can only get me so far, you know?"

He could do it, Velvet mused. He could look hilarious if he tried.

"You got something there," Velvet cheered him on.

Domino took his bows and walked off, dragging his tail on the floor in a pattern that revealed the words, *Thanks for the memories*.

"Awe," Velvet sighed. Mikey did too, but it could have been about the jumbo deluxe banana split she handed him.

Being home felt good. A swim with her sister felt even better. Noelia looked stunning in her golden tail, silver and gold shells, and gold-colored hair. She was wearing long nails painted to match her top.

"Did you dress up for me?" Velvet asked, kissing her on the cheek.

Noelia posed against Riddle's sandcastle. "It's for my new author photo. We took the pictures this morning. What do you think?"

"I think you look marvelous. Gold and silver are good on you. Is it okay if I joke about it?" Velvet was already looking for new material for her next act.

"Why, does it look funny to you?" Noelia pulled a mirror from nowhere and examined herself for flaws.

"Not at all, but I'm a comedian, remember? I'm only asking in case I can make jokes out of it. You know I don't like to hurt anyone's feelings with my act."

"That's sweet of you, but leave me out of it, okay? This is my author photo we're talking about. It's important to me."

They had vastly different styles, but in the end, they wanted the same thing; to entertain. Velvet agreed with a nod.

"So, how was it? It feels like you were gone forever." Noelia swam away from the sandcastle subtly, but Velvet knew that she wanted to be as far from Riddle as possible. His appearance made her uncomfortable.

They'd had too many discussions about why Velvet chose to live in his sandcastle when there was no reason for her to. At least, that was Noelia's opinion.

Velvet saw a sweetness in Riddle, in the way he helped people in the World and creatures in the Dreaming that drew her to him. He was a creative and thoughtful friend.

Time was a relative way of looking at things in the Dreaming. Creatures could observe it or ignore it. In this case, Velvet agreed with Noelia that it felt like it had been a while since they were together before she left for the tour.

"It was sensational. I've never had so many laughs. There may be another one coming up, which is why I'm writing new jokes. I'll keep my big laughs from the other acts, and add a few new ones. How are you?"

"I'm..."

Velvet gave her sister time to find the right words. They called one another sister because they chose to, but since creatures weren't born to families the way that people, animals, and so on, were in the World, it was a term of endearment. Sister was an idea that came from the World. Not all creatures knew what it meant.

Today was one of those days when Noelia didn't know what she was doing with her life. With herself. With anything.

"In need of a hug, I'd say." Velvet followed up with open arms. Noelia floated into them and gripped tightly.

Velvet held Noelia while the gorgeous creature took deep, calming breaths. "I felt lost while you were away," Noelia said. Velvet held on until Noelia was ready to let go.

"Better?" Velvet asked, patting Noelia on the shoulder.

"Much. You always know what to do. I guess that's why we chose to be sisters."

Noelia's appreciation made Velvet feel wonderful. "Good taste runs in the family."

"Thank you." Noelia bowed.

The sisters spent the rest of their afternoon chatting, exploring the water, and stopping to visit with creatures they knew along the way. Velvet wondered if Noelia would elaborate on what had upset her, but the subject never came up again. Maybe all Noelia needed was time with her.

The sisters hugged and then parted to go back to their homes, feeling one hundred percent refreshed from their time together.

Chapter 5

Velvet visited with her dear friend Riddle for most of the next morning. He showed her the history he had added to his sandcastle walls while she was away on the tour.

One of the designs was a story from a world she hadn't seen before. She suspected that it was where Riddle, and possibly Debra, came from originally.

The story was about happy, content, creatures practicing the art of creating, sometimes with teachers, and at other times on their own. The final, cleverly painted frame of the story depicted the accomplishment of a luxurious looking natural world, full of wildlife, lush green trees, and crystal blue waters.

"This is a beautiful story." Velvet planted a kiss on the top of Riddle's head.

He blushed, as she thought he might. There were times when she held her kisses back so she wouldn't embarrass him. She enjoyed his new art too much to hold back this time.

"Thank you." Riddle mumbled, and then cleared his throat.

"Can I ask questions about it?" She'd learned long ago to respect Riddle's privacy and wouldn't push the point if he was reluctant.

Riddle didn't hesitate. Apparently he already decided what he was willing to share about the story.

"You may have one. Then your questions will be done."

He didn't always speak in rhyme, but the few who were lucky enough to know him knew that when he did, he was imparting a true gift. Few people knew Riddle at all. Even fewer had heard him speak.

One question. Velvet pondered. The perfect question then popped into her head.

"What does this story mean to you?" Velvet settled onto a chair while Riddle looked from her, to the picture, and then back again.

"It means that we all have a greater gift than we realize. We can create infinitely more than we give ourselves credit for." Riddle settled himself into a chair like Velvet's, and then smiled at her when he saw that she understood how much he meant what he said.

"Thank you for sharing this with me, Riddle. It means a lot to me that you did."

Riddle simply smiled. They sat together in companionable silence until Velvet decided to try a few of her new physical comedy jokes on him.

Riddle smiled and clapped. He looked giddy. Seeing Riddle acting so happy was one of the best feelings Velvet had felt or imagined.

Long ago, Velvet had knocked on the sandcastle door with the simple goal of telling the creature who lived there that she thought it was an incredible looking sandcastle.

The door had opened on its own, and Velvet stepped inside without hesitation.

She thought Riddle took a chance in allowing a new creature into his home, considering his reclusive nature, but his intuition was much more developed than Velvet understood at the time.

When she saw him for the first time, and accepted him completely through her reactions, they became friends.

Their friendship was one of the closest and most important in both of their lives.

VELVET VISITED THE Hall of Records next, eagerly running through scenarios of who her mystery vistor was.

Could he be an explorer from the World, who was too frightened by the creatures he saw to continue?

Could his visits to the Dreaming be a fun new game her friend You was playing with her? You was usually a busy spirit guide, so she didn't think it was likely that he was playing an elaborate joke with her.

The Hall of Records was a large white building that sat by itself. It admitted anyone whom it felt had a legitimate reason to be there. Velvet had not seen any creatures turned away from the Hall, but she had heard stories.

It was said that if you intended to harm someone with the information found in the Hall, you would not be allowed in.

There was even a rumor that there was a creature trapped somewhere in the Hall, because the Hall decided that the information they learned was too dangerous to be let out into the Dreaming.

Velvet loved that story and had spent chunks of time looking around the Hall, knocking on walls and being noisy, to encourage the captive to clue her in on their position. So far, she hadn't found anything. The adventure was her favorite mystery.

First, Velvet planned to search the written archives and asked to see all of the records about the visitor.

The Hall of Records was enormous. Velvet navigated it the way she usually did, gliding down the long hallways, across the large, ornately decorated rooms. She felt a sense of peace in the rooms, so prevalent it reached through her extreme anticipation.

She felt at home in the Hall; probably because she spent so much time there.

Crossing the last threshold from the gray hallway into the written archives room furnished with plush maroon-colored couches, she wasted no time in telling the Hall about her meetings with him, and showed it a picture of him from her memory.

Velvet sighed her disappointment when a single page floated into her hands. The only word printed on the page was Saunders.

"Is this his name?" Velvet inquired.

The word yes appeared directly under Saunders on her paper.

"Is there anything about him in the photo or video room?" Velvet took deep breaths to calm her frustration. The Hall didn't like to be pushed around by a creature's feelings.

The Hall was in good humor today, because instead of directing her to the photo room, it showed her a photo of a lonely-looking cabin in a snowy white field.

"Is this where Saunders lives?" Velvet asked the Hall.

Nothing about this investigation was going the way it usually did, because if a visitor was in the Dreaming, there was a record of them in the Hall.

The word yes highlighted on the page in her hand.

Velvet's intuition that Saunders was a visitor to the Dreaming intensified. "Is this cabin in the World?"

The word yes highlighted on the page in her hand again.

"Is there anything about Saunders in the video room?" *I wonder what kind of name Saunders is.*

The word no appeared beneath the yes on the paper she held in her hands.

Without asking, Velvet knew that the Hall had shown her everything it knew about Saunders. She asked anyway. "Is there any more information about Saunders?"

The word *no* glowed on her paper.

She felt complete knowing that the Hall shared all that it could, and empty that she hadn't learned more from her visit.

"Thank you." Velvet told the Hall, purposely infusing deep gratitude into the words. "I appreciate all that you do for me, and for other creatures, and visitors."

The mystery deepened. Why wasn't there more information about Saunders?

Velvet made her way back to the Hall entrance and then sat on the steps, thinking. There was only one constant between the two times she had seen Saunders; a dark patch of water unlike any she had seen before. She was determined now to find another one of those patches.

Unlike the other areas she had explored during the tour, Velvet knew this part of the Dreaming intimately. Now, where to start. She tapped her tail on the stairs, picturing her favorite spots, and the ones she didn't spend as much time in.

Decided, she headed directly to an older part of the Dreaming, swimming quickly and waving briefly to friends she passed by.

They would wonder about that since she always had time for a chat.

As she neared the ship graveyard, Velvet slowed down enough to be able to see the colors in the water. There were a lot of different shades of blue, and green, and one dark patch. Funny how she hadn't noted the color differences before.

Her heart thumped with excitement as she entered the dark patch, fully prepared to see Saunders and try to talk with him.

Her delight in seeing him rapidly faded when she saw how sad and lost he looked where he sat on the edge of the deck of a large ship, his long legs hanging over the side.

Based on their past meetings, Velvet wanted to reassure him so he wouldn't panic and swim away.

"Saunders." She called his name in a gentle voice. "Please don't be afraid. I'm Velvet. Remember me? We've seen one another twice before."

She waited, letting him take in her words as he looked slowly up and around to where she floated.

"How do you know my name?"

She hadn't realized that she was expecting him to run away again until it was clear to her that he was willing to talk with her this time. She stayed where she was and answered, "I learned it in the Hall of Records. It's a building here in the Dreaming where you can research almost anything." Before her experience researching him, she would have said you could research anything there.

"The Dreaming! So I am dreaming. This is a dream world!" Saunders punched the water in his excitement.

It was Velvet's turn to think. No, she shook her head. She couldn't be a dream. If her world was only a dream, then that would mean that it existed only when someone was dreaming it. She, and her world, existed all the time. Otherwise someone would have to be dreaming them all the time, wouldn't they?

Her research in the Hall had taught her that the Dreaming was created as a paradise for those who embraced magic. Nothing in her research even suggested that they weren't real.

"I... I don't know what to say to that. I am not a dream. I am not asleep. Creatures don't even sleep here. The only reason I know what sleep is, is because of entertainments I've watched in the archives in the Hall of Records."

"Velvet," he said gently, "I'm trying to understand what's happening to me. In no way am I trying to hurt your feelings. You're the only...creature...who has tried to talk to me. I don't know how I got here. Why I'm here. I barely know my name."

A huge, beautiful smile lit her face. "I know that you are a visitor, and that usually visitors are sleeping when they visit here, so if you want to say that this is a dream world, for you, I think that's okay."

"Good. So, what is there to do here?" Saunders looked below himself, then behind himself, and then to where Velvet had swam from. "If I'm stuck here, I may as well try to enjoy it."

"Do you like comedy?" Velvet couldn't help herself. She wanted her new friend to like what she was most passionate about. "I'm a comedian, and so are many of my friends. We could go watch a performance!" Velvet's irrepressible enthusiasm instantly broke through the odd feelings their last two meetings put between them.

"A comedy show? I could use a laugh, and I don't know what else there is to do."

"Excellent! If you'll hold my hand, I can take us to the show."

"You're not shy, are you?" He took the hand she offered.

Chapter 6

Her hand felt solid in his. Holding hands. On their way to a comedy show. *Is this a date?*

Saunders didn't want to spoil the experience, but he had to ask – "Why do we need to hold hands? Is it to anchor me here?"

The question flustered her. He could tell by the way she froze where they were and wrinkled her brow. "I – I don't like how much I don't know. I used to think I was a knowledgeable creature, but your questions have been stumping me. Why would you need to be anchored?"

That wasn't what I asked. Why doesn't she answer the question? He waited, watching her.

They hadn't moved far from the ship graveyard. The water was warm around him. The bottom of the ocean would be cold if it wasn't a dream. And he'd be dead. Maybe this was the afterlife.

Holding hands in the silence started to feel awkward. She must have agreed because she released his hand.

"I guess we could swim to the club together like this." She clasped her hands together and held them at her bare midriff. Her bottom lip trembled.

Damn, he'd hurt her feelings. "I'm trying to understand. That's all."

She must have believed him, because her infectious smile was back. "You need clothes. What do you want to wear?"

They both looked at his lower half. *At least I like what I see. I've been naked this whole time and didn't even realize it.*

"Shorts, I guess? A shirt? What do visitors wear?"

"Do you like this?" She pointed to his chest and legs, where a black shirt and red shorts appeared.

"They fit, so yeah. I can wear this. And I'm not naked."

She laughed. "I always wear a tail."

But no shells. He liked her sexy look and how calm and friendly she was.

"Do you want to go watch the show?" She pointed off in the distance.

When was the last time he'd let go and had fun? He couldn't remember. He didn't think he was known for his manners, but he'd already been rude to her when she'd been nice to him from the beginning. "I'd like that."

He swam beside her, watching the way she sliced through the water with her fin.

They were at the club door in what felt like minutes. The swan at the door knew Velvet by name and told her that her usual table was available.

"Do you like to sit in the front?" She asked, pointing to a table for two.

"Why not?" He didn't know the real answer and he was starting to understand how much he couldn't remember. *What happened to me?*

A panda came to take their drink order after they sat down.

"I don't want anything. Tell Pearson what you want," Velvet said.

Saunders didn't know what to ask for. "You pick."

"My friends like Champagne. Let's get that."

"Okay. Champagne, please."

The panda was still looking at Velvet. "Saunders would like a glass of Champagne."

The panda shrugged and walked away. It returned with a full glass of the pale, sparkling drink and a cocktail napkin, setting both on the table in front of Velvet.

"Thank you, but it's for him." Velvet slid the glass over.

This time the panda laughed and patted Velvet on the shoulder. "Good one."

"Good what?" She asked, but the panda was already talking to guests at the table two rows behind them.

The place was almost full, but her table was reserved for her. "Did they know you would be here?" He asked.

She shook her head. "I was looking for you. We're lucky they had a table."

The crowd around them laughed when the two fluorescent orange squids on stage pointed at Velvet. The spotlight was blinding when it landed on Velvet and Saunders.

"Give it up for Velvet and her new routine. We didn't know you could act like that. You should be an actress and a comedian."

"Act like what?" Velvet asked, but they had started their next joke.

Saunders wondered what they were talking about, too, all the way up until he found himself in a freezing, snowy white field, with a familiar cabin off in the distance. The cabin must be important because he kept ending up there, but he had no idea why.

He had a nagging feeling that he should know more about the cabin, and the spot where he stood staring at it.

Instead of puzzling out why he was there, he yelled his frustration to the vast emptiness surrounding him. "Where is the water? Bring me back to the water!"

When nothing changed around him, he called out, "Velvet, where are you?"

He sat in the snow to wait, this time hoping that Velvet would appear. He sat with the snow falling steadily on his shoulders, until it covered his lap. Dry snow, he mused. Snow wasn't even wet here.

He stood, brushing the powder off. He was going to try and walk to the cabin. Why hadn't he tried to go to it before? He shrugged his shoulders and started his trudge forward.

His legs felt cumbersome, like they weighed hundreds of pounds. Exhausted after only a few steps, he stopped and measured his progress. He wasn't any closer to the cabin.

He struggled to remember what he was doing before he found Velvet the last time, but there wasn't even a hint of memory.

Chapter 7

Saunders disappeared from Velvet's side. In an instant, his chair sat empty.

Velvet turned to the creatures seated at the next table, asking, "Did you see where my friend went?"

The three creatures looked at one another and burst out laughing. The smallest of the three, an octopus, shook his head no. "If I wasn't sitting here from the time you sat down I would totally believe you had someone with you."

Velvet's smile fell. She touched the chair Saunders was sitting in and enjoyed the warmth that proved he had been there with her. Her joy faded as fast as the heat on the chair seat.

"Thank you," she mumbled. It wasn't their fault she was having so many troubles with her new friend.

CASSIDY FOUND VELVET in her room a long time later, sitting on a chair, flapping her tail rhythmically against the sandy floor. Cassidy sought her out because she hadn't heard from Velvet until she cancelled her long-standing performance two nights ago.

"What's going on, Velvet? Please tell me you haven't been here alone all this time."

She invited Cassidy to sit on the couch by pointing.

With no new information about Saunders in the Hall of Records and fruitless searching for him, she had given up.

Velvet knew her friends were worried. She was worried, too. Worried about Saunders. She knew he existed because the Hall had a record of him. That was her only comfort.

She had searched the spots where they were together and couldn't find even one creature who had seen him.

No dark water signified his presence, as it had before. She was out of ideas.

"Velvet?" Cassidy tried again, concern making her name sound like a plea.

Velvet shook herself and forced her attention onto her friend and manager. "I'm sorry. I do have a problem. Maybe you could help with it." *Why didn't I think of that before*? Talking with her friends about what was happening in her life was one of her favorite things to do.

Forgetting to talk to her friends was another sign that she was far from normal.

Cassidy listened while Velvet described her meetings with Saunders, her research in the Hall of Records, and how she found him again.

Velvet was embarrassed to admit that no one else had seen him, including the audience at the comedy show.

"I wish I could say that I have an idea that would help you with finding Saunders. Visitors have always been rare, but when they are here, everyone I know can see them. I've never seen you so down."

"What do I do? I can't stop thinking about it. About Saunders." She heard the sadness and desperation in her voice.

She also couldn't stop feeling the difference between how she felt when she was spending time with him, and now. He took all the color and joy with him.

"Maybe I can help. How about a juicy primetime slot at a new club? Would you like that? I came over to check on you and to share the news. Performing could be what you need. Check this out."

Cassidy held a photograph of The Pearl, the second most popular club in all of the Dreaming. Velvet's name was on the marquee.

Velvet paused thumping her tail. "I appreciate that you're trying so hard to lift my spirits. Before this," she waved her hand around, "I would have been ecstatic to see my name on their marquee."

"I'll do whatever you need to feel better. Is this it? I don't want you to feel worse."

"I can't feel worse than this. Tell them I'll do it."

VELVET'S HANDS TREMBLED from opening night jitters. If she couldn't get some life and color into her routine, no one was going to laugh when she was on stage. Or at least not the way she wanted them to.

She waited in the wings while the comedian before her drew a few weak laughs from a sober crowd.

Not a good sign for her.

Lefty was the name of the act in front of her. Based on what she was seeing, she was going to try a whole new approach. This crowd needed what she hadn't dared to give any crowd before.

"Good luck, sister!" Lefty told her sarcastically as he walked by her on his way out the back door.

"It gets better," Velvet called after him. "Don't give up!"

She wished she could take her own advice. Instead, she wore bravado like it was a new outfit she should love, then discovered it didn't fit just as she walked out onto the stage.

At least the microphone felt solid in her hand.

She chose a happy looking couple in the audience and dove into joking about what was putting the smile on their faces.

They liked it. The rest of the crowd liked it, and the fact that she was picking on someone else. *That wouldn't last long.* She chose another table to joke with. Four men out for a night on the town.

Teasing the couple about sex worked well. Teasing the guys about what kind of broad they would meet in a comedy club worked, too.

A quick glance to where Cassidy sat at the back of the room proved that she wasn't fooling herself or Cassidy, but the crowd cheered for more.

At the end of the night when she and Cassidy were alone in the back of the limo Cassidy manifested, Velvet listened to praise she knew she deserved.

"Points for guts. You've never gone after the tables like that before."

"I knew they needed shaking up. Poor Lefty. His jokes were tight."

"Yeah, they did. Listen, you've taken time off, and now you're back. Why don't we plan on you finishing this gig. They want you to stay for two more shows. Don't say no."

Velvet shrugged. "I'll stay. What else would I do?"

"Come stay at my place. I've been collecting a new show about a wannabe comedian's wife being funnier than her husband. You're going to love it. It'll remind you of when you got your first laugh from an audience."

Velvet gave a small nod to agree and settled back into the seat cushion, looking for dark spots outside the window. One hand was pressed against the door handle in case she saw one.

Chapter 8

After countless standout performances, Velvet was still having trouble enjoying her success, when she could see the point of any of it at all.

It was bad enough for Riddle to be visibly concerned about her. She was being honest when she told him she appreciated his concern. She was close to asking him to intervene – which meant she was past desperate for answers. Or progress. For Saunders, who mattered most of all. *I hope he's safe.*

She roused herself from the couch, thinking she imagined sounds coming from her door. She had only left her room to perform lately and hadn't been much of a companion to anyone. No one knew what to do for her, so visits from friends had stopped a while ago.

"Yes?" She called out, testing.

"It's me, Velvet. I hoped we could talk."

"Oh, Riddle!" She threw the door open and grabbed her short friend in a tight hug. "I haven't been a good friend to you recently. You know it's not about you."

Riddle awkwardly tried to comfort her with tentative touches on her arm. Touching other creatures was difficult and immensely uncomfortable for him under any circumstance.

He blushed. "You have been having a hard time. I understand that. I wish I could do more for you. That is why I bring you this."

She let go of their hug and stepped back to see what he brought. He offered her what looked like a closed clam shell.

"Uh, thanks." She accepted the gift, trying to hide her confusion.

"It holds a message. From me." Riddle stepped back, turned, and rushed from the room.

She was touched that Riddle would share a message with her. He was selective about how he shared his incredible knowledge.

She sat on the edge of her bed and looked carefully at the shell in her hand. She couldn't find a button to press. The shell remained closed.

"Open sesame," Velvet told the shell in a joking voice. Then she wiggled her fingers at it and said, "Alakazam and hocus pocus."

No luck, even with two magic words and sarcasm. Audiences were easier than clam shells.

Velvet placed the shell gently on the bed and stared at it until she felt unbearably drawn to a dream. She curled her fin to her stomach and let it come.

In her dream, she swam with a whole sea filled with Saunders. She could reach out and feel them. She tried to kiss the one closest to her and found that he was more than willing to experiment with her. She hugged him close, afraid he would disappear. Which of course he did. It was only a dream. She knew that.

As she woke, Velvet heard the message clearly from the shell. Riddle's voice. "In this world, lost and confused, salvation lies in choice."

The message had to be for Saunders. He had a choice to make. *I wonder what it is. And why can't he see it? Or did he already and that's why I can't find him? Why is everything so complicated for us?*

She swam out of her room to thank Riddle for his message, pausing long enough to knock once on his doorframe.

"You're the best friend a creature can have," she told him, giving him an air kiss near his cheek. There was no way to kiss him without embarrassing him, and that wasn't what she wanted at all. "I needed this boost. To know that there's hope for Saunders, even when I didn't talk to you about him."

"I wanted to cheer you up and I had information he needs to get through...That's all I can tell you."

"If everyone knew how much you care, they would shower you with gifts." She saw the concern on his face and rushed to reassure him. "I won't tell anyone, Riddle. Your secret is safe with me. I only wanted to tell you how grateful I am."

Riddle nodded and started walking backward to his main room. He spent most of his time there, pondering. She suspected he spent his time thinking across worlds and realities others only guessed existed.

Velvet let him go, and then rushed out to look for a dark spot with renewed purpose. She could finally make a difference for Saunders. If she could find him. If he wanted to be found.

If she wasn't tireless and didn't care how many oceans she had to search before she found the dark spot, she would have given up long before she found him.

When she saw him, he was sitting on the fine sand of a lonely, deserted island with one palm tree to lean against.

Velvet smiled in relief for the first time since the last time she was with him. Then she created a coconut with a smiling face, hid it behind her back, and showed herself to Saunders.

"Velvet! Is that really you this time?"

The confusion she felt about his question crossed her face, and then disappeared when she reached him and shyly offered him the smooth coconut.

"If you're not real, you'll disappear like the others when I touch you." He put a hand on her arm, then slid his fingers down to her fingers, finally holding both of his hands over hers. The coconut fell to the sand.

"I gave up for a while," she admitted in a quiet voice. "I couldn't find you, and the only proof I had that I didn't make you up was in the Hall of Records."

"I didn't even have the option of looking for you, or not looking for you. I end up wherever I am and hope that you're going to be there. Why is this happening to me?" He squeezed her hand, then let it go. "I didn't mean to sound like I'm angry with you. You deserve better."

"I don't know what's happening to you, but my friend gave me a message for you."

She handed him the clam shell, which played Riddle's message when he held it in his palm.

"I don't know what this means, do you?" He shook the shell. "In case there's more in there." He sat on the sand, patting the spot next to him. "Do you want to sit?"

"I was hoping you knew what it meant. What were you asking before, about if it's me *this time*?" She settled onto the sand to sit next to him. Her tail pointed toward him.

"There have been...illusions. They look like you, but when I touch them, there's nothing there. It's been happening for a while. They can't talk, either. Have you been seeing illusions of me?"

"Once, in a dream. I'd like to know what your illusions mean. If there's a way to find out, let's do it. If there isn't and you've been miserable like I have, then let's have fun. What do you want to do?"

His smile made her fin flutter.

"If you don't think we can find answers, then let's go enjoy ourselves. Maybe I should hold onto your hand, so we won't be separated again."

She wanted to hold his hand. "I went to the Hall of Records and asked if there was information there for you. The Hall said no. I can't think of where we can go for more information, so let's go to one of my favorite spots. The sea grass grows tall and there are small, friendly creatures who wear green hats. Swim on your back so we can watch the creatures floating above us."

Saunders turned to float on his back the way she was.

They weren't far from the little island when she pointed to what looked like fluorescent blue peace signs, dancing, and leaving a bright trail in the water.

Chapter 9

"I wish I wasn't tired." Saunders yawned. "You have so many interesting places you want to show me." His favorites so far were castles, dinosaurs, submarines, and breathtaking islands with stunning waterfalls. She was full of adventure and had endless enthusiastic ideas.

They were laying on the wings of a giant blue butterfly. He was on the left one, she was on the right. Floating in mid-air was smooth and graceful. He was surprised when they first saw the butterfly on a huge sunflower, but that was nothing compared to when it asked Velvet if she wanted a ride, which she said she'd never done before. He had accepted that Velvet was the only creature who could see him and wasn't surprised the butterfly didn't acknowledge him even after he walked onto its wing.

"I wonder what tired feels like," Velvet said.

"You want to be tired? Wow, that's a weird thought. So you're never tired and you never sleep. I wondered if you were making a special effort for me."

"I know that some people in the World wish they didn't need to sleep. Then they could work all the time. I wonder what work is like."

"What you do is work. I think that in the World you would be paid to tell jokes if you were as popular there as you are here."

They had done so much in their time together, talking, exploring, sharing, and shyly flirting, that he was afraid of what would happen to her if he disappeared. He was storing memories in case she was taken from him again.

"Right, like Lucy Ricardo and that funny family on Raising Hope. Comedy is more popular in the World than it is here, I think."

"You'd know the answer to that better than I could because you know more about the World than I do, and you're certain I'm from there. All I know is that watching your show the past few times has been a blast for me. I think you're happiest when you're performing."

"There's no reason to be serious all the time. I want to make creatures laugh."

But he did have to be serious, at least long enough to talk about what neither of them wanted to admit. "I need to talk about what could happen if I leave again. Please, tell me you'll do your best to stay happy if that happens. I can't stand the thought of hurting you."

She assured him that she would, but he saw and felt her sadness. Plus she changed the subject.

She said, "Let's go to Sky Park now. We can sit on the moon and watch the stars light up."

He wouldn't deny her the chance to go to her favorite place. The fatigue wouldn't go away. It had to mean there was a change coming. He wouldn't have objected even if he had control over where he was because he liked Sky Park, too.

They sat on a moon and watched the stars light up, soaking in the magical sights. It was romantic. Purple moonlight highlighted Velvet's pale, petal-soft skin.

"I have to tell you something," he said. He cupped her cheeks with his hands and gently turned her face to his.

"What?" She asked, meeting his gaze.

Her perfect face, her luminous, beautiful eyes, were mesmerizing. He was transfixed by the feelings swirling around them. He leaned forward and placed a soft kiss on her lips.

She moved closer and hugged him tight, deepening the kiss.

He made himself pull away to say, "I... I think you should know that I like you a lot."

"I like you a lot, too. I like spending time with you."

Her words were simple, but the emotion in her body language filled in the magnitude of what she left unsaid.

"Me, too." He breathed out a sigh of relief. He knew that they had a solid friendship, but the kiss was risky. Their flirting was light and playful. She'd never made a serious move on him.

She sighed and snuggled into his side.

Saunders put his right arm around her slender shoulders and watched the glow from the nearest green star light up her face. "You look good in the moon and starlight."

"I was starting to think you didn't think of me as more than a friend. I guess I could have lived with that, but I'm so much happier knowing that you like me, too."

He chuckled, then asked, "Were you going to tell me?"

She shrugged, then pointed out a rainbow star streaking through the water. "I don't know. Thinking about what would happen if you didn't feel the same way...I didn't want to push you away."

"I understand." Saunders finished the words with another big yawn. This time he tried to fool himself into thinking he could find a way around his lethargy.

"Why don't we go back to where I stay so you can rest?"

She blushed when she said that. Interesting. He nodded. "I appreciate it."

They swam through warm water, holding hands and sharing laughter-filled glances.

Creatures they passed thought Velvet was looking at them, which brought up questions he was determined to ask. Right then, he was feeling dirty because he was watching her hair to see if it would shift and show him her bare breasts. How did she keep them covered all the time?

He wasn't ready to ask.

As soon as it started, Saunders knew he was losing her again. The bright, clear water was replaced with endless miles of snow and trees. "No!" He shouted, hearing the sound echo all around him.

He heard her shout and saw her grab for his hand. He reached for hers, defeated when his fingers went through hers. He called her name but judging from the look on her face she didn't hear him.

Then she was gone.

Chapter 10

ENDLESS GLISTENING snow. The distant cabin. The tree line. He expected to see them, but who were the woman, the little boy, and the dog running toward him?

There was a vague sense of familiarity, but not enough to understood why she greeted him with enthusiastic hugs and kisses.

"Darling!" The woman said as she covered his face with more kisses. "Where have you been? We thought we'd be with you right away."

Lucky for Saunders she didn't seem to need for him to say anything. *Where would I even start with my questions?*

"Look, Dad, I found Sparky!"

The boy summoned a huge, floppy-eared, white mop of a dog, who came running.

Saunders knelt with the boy to pet the dog, testing. The dog felt solid. The woman had, too. Sparky acted like they knew each other.

"Thomas," the woman knelt with them, "I'm so glad you found Sparky. And now we have Daddy."

Thomas looked like the woman, their faces sunburnt, from what he could see peeking through their hooded jackets. They had brown eyes and freckles.

She turned smiling, loving eyes to look into his. Saunders turned his head, because he knew that she wasn't going to like what she saw.

She whispered, "It's okay." She soothed him with her words and a brush of her fingers on his hand. "It's been a long time."

A name floated into his mind. Diane.

"Diane?" he whispered. He still couldn't turn his face to hers. He obviously meant a lot to her and his whole focus was set on getting back to Velvet as soon as he could.

She nodded. Tears flowed down her cheeks. She placed a gentle hand over his left one and squeezed.

The ring on the fourth finger of his left hand hadn't been there before this return to the mystery field. What did that mean? *Who are Diane, Thomas, and Sparky?*

Saunders closed his eyes to try and sort through his jumbled thoughts. The ring was important. Daddy was important.

"James," Diane whispered, "I'll take Thomas and Sparky into the house. You need time to, oh, I don't know. You aren't happy to see us." Diane huffed out a breath of cold air and turned to call Thomas and Sparky to go with her.

James? There are two things I know for sure. My name is Saunders and I want to be with Velvet.

He kept his eyes closed, opening them when he sensed things had changed. Again. When he opened his eyes he was alone.

He sat in the snow long after Diane, Thomas, and Sparky disappeared. There was no way to get closer to the cabin, where he assumed they went.

He turned away from the cabin and started walking, only this time, he walked in the direction of the white field. There were no mountains or trees in that direction. In fact, he wasn't sure he had seen this desolate place before.

Snow that wasn't cold or wet. What *was the point of it*? He didn't even know if this was part of the Dreaming.

A new sound reached his ears. Running water. He rushed toward it, noticing that the snow wasn't as deep where he was going.

There, in the distance, was a flowing stream. As he moved closer, he saw a figure lying there. His hope that it was Velvet was immediately dashed; the figure was too large to be her.

He started running, tears falling down his cheeks, because part of him knew, somehow, what he was going to see when he was close enough.

With a ragged breath he stopped and looked at himself, lying in pebbly sand a foot away from the snow. His eyes were closed. His hands, clenched.

He screamed in frustration. "What? What the hell is going on? Why am I here? What the hell is happening to me?" He exhausted his rage and then crumpled down beside his body.

There was a large wound on his head. He was completely still. Tentatively, he touched the jacket. He was half afraid that the body would move, and half afraid that it wouldn't.

Tears continued to fall from his eyes as memories surfaced of the day he walked from his cabin to the stream to catch more fish.

He remembered that the cabin he retreated to a year before was where he went when his daily life lost its meaning. Memories flew through his mind with astonishing speed, but there were still too many blanks.

He was a robot then, going through the motions of working, eating, and sleeping.

Fresh, soul-wrenching tears fell onto the ground beside him as he tried to remember who Diane, Thomas, and Sparky were to him. Had he abandoned his family?

He urgently tried to recall memories of them, grunting in frustration when he couldn't think of any others. They said they had waited for him for so long...

The fishing pole laid beside him. Blood on the slippery, moss-covered rock near his feet answered a lot of what he was wondering.

He must be in a place between the world of the living and Velvet's world.

Chapter 11

Saunders forced himself to sit next to his still body while his brain remembered the crushing numbness that drove him away from his business before there was nothing left to value in life.

The cabin was just over the hill behind him and he knew why he bought it now. To immerse himself in solitude. For how long, he hadn't planned. He only knew that being with other people was the last thing he wanted. So he bought a cabin in the middle of nowhere.

A cabin he hadn't been able to get back to because he was bleeding in the snow on the riverbank.

The first happiness he'd felt in years was the time he'd spent with Velvet. He didn't care if that made him seem crazy, or if he was crazy.

Rising to his feet, he walked away from the freezing cold water. To where, he didn't know. This place was so quiet.

He wished Velvet was there. He needed to talk with her, even if he had no idea what he would say. He already missed how alive he felt when they were together.

Now that was ironic.

He hung his head as he walked, watching his feet take one step, and then another, until he saw the bottom step that led to his cabin.

Why could he reach his cabin now, when he'd been trying for so long? What. Had. Changed?

He braced himself to face Diane, Thomas, and Sparky. The last time he saw them they were headed there, and they weren't outside.

His cabin smelled the way he knew it should; like smoky residue from the cold fireplace and oranges from the open can of juice sitting on the counter. Stacks of logs waited next to the fireplace.

There was a blue pickup truck he could see through the kitchen window.

There was no sign of the woman, the boy, or the dog. No wedding ring on his finger.

He glanced at the bed, the large, green circular rug on the wood floor, the kitchen he used only to open cans and eat what was inside. This was what he'd been calling life.

As his gaze touched on his few belongings, he felt drawn to the table with one lonely chair. There were papers and books there. Information, at last.

What this place had in common with the Dreaming was timelessness. He had no way of knowing how long it took between the time he picked up the first letter on the desk to when he placed the final one upside down onto the pile.

For the last year he'd been living there, isolated, by his own choice. He'd accomplished enough in his life to be able to do that. The letters from his assistant told him that all was well with his businesses and they hoped he would return soon.

The mystery of who Diane, Thomas, and Sparky were was solved. His brain did weird things with the novel he'd been reading on the morning he went to the stream.

His journal was the most interesting, revealing how his existence became empty.

The thrill of succeeding in his businesses after growing up a poor foster child faded years before. He'd never felt like he fit in.

His first success was earning enough money to take care of himself; to make his own rules. To be his own person.

Then he'd worked hard in construction because it paid well and he was good at it. He'd lived frugally, saving everything he could, until he had enough to get his contractor's license and insurance.

One by one, he added workers to his crew until he could cover all the bases for his satisfied commercial and residential customers. Referrals flowed in. His contracts and his crews grew.

When he had a profitable company, he bought a car dealership. That was when the serious money happened.

Until the large numbers in his bank account lost meaning. That's when he'd gone to the secluded cabin in the woods to figure out what he wanted for himself.

His personal life didn't exist. At first women couldn't compare to the highs of building his empire.

Memories came back to him of boring dinners with decadently beautiful women sitting by his side. He spent the whole night thinking about work and pretending interest, at first. After a while, he gave up the pretense and was openly distracted. His companions didn't care. He was giving them what they wanted; to be seen with him. Dined by him. Involved with him. But there was no love there. No excitement.

He'd looked for a spark to take him in a new direction. Now he'd found it. It had taken a year and a nasty crack on the head, but he knew what he wanted. Velvet. The only question was, how could he make it so that they could stay together?

Saunders walked back to the stream, hoping for more clarity. Being near the water reminded him of her.

The clamshell message said that his salvation would come from choice. If he understood what was happening to him, it meant that he would no longer have any life in this world. When he didn't email his assistant to tell him he had received his latest package the man would ask the sheriff to check on him. His body would be found. There would be a funeral. That world was taken care of.

He was free to be with Velvet. Right now. All he had to do was figure out how to get back to her.

His fervent wishing created a multitude of fake Velvets, which he waved away with a swipe of his hand. They weren't vibrant enough to be her.

Maybe I have to announce my choice. "I choose to be with Velvet," Saunders yelled as loud as he could.

His words were absorbed by the snow.

Chapter 12

VELVET SWAM WITH NOELIA, stopping to chat with creatures they knew. It was a gorgeous day in the Dreaming. Velvet's spirits were higher now because she comforted herself with the thought that she had given Saunders Riddle's clue, and hoped Saunders had found his way. They were friends, and friends helped each other.

Velvet saw Noelia glance at the dark spots of water appearing around them.

"What is this, Velvet?" Noelia stopped swimming and pointed to the dark water patches growing thicker until they obliterated the clear blue water they were used to.

"It's..." Velvet paused, looking for a way around the dark patches. They were walled in. She panicked when she didn't see any blue water around them to escape to. It was okay to want the best for him, wherever he was, but to spend time with him in a platonic friendship... No. She wasn't ready for that.

"Velvet!" Saunders called out, swimming toward them.

"Who is that?" Noelia asked.

Noelia could see him now?

Velvet tried to look casual while she looked for a way out of the dark water.

"I found you! I- What's wrong?" He asked.

There was no escape for Velvet. The joy she felt from being near Saunders again lit her up until Noelia had to pull her eyes away from Saunders to remark about it.

"Um, Velvet, you're glowing." Noelia said. "He is, too."

"This," Velvet sighed, "is Saunders. The visitor I told you about."

"I'm the previously invisible man." He waved at Noelia.

"We have to talk. But first I should introduce you to Noelia, my sister."

"Charmed," Noelia murmured silkily, offering her hand for him to kiss.

Velvet wasn't even annoyed by her sister's flirting. That was who Noelia was.

He politely accepted Noelia's hand, and shook it.

"Do you want me to go?" Noelia asked Velvet.

"I think Saunders and I need to talk this out. I'll see you later." Velvet hugged Noelia.

"Later." Noelia waved and swam away.

"Velvet." He put a hand on her arm.

She wanted to be angry with him for taking most of the joy from her world when he disappeared. Why couldn't she hold on to a tiny piece of that anger? Just this once?

"Could we go somewhere quiet?" He pointed to the creatures swimming around them, watching, and listening in. "I have a lot to tell you."

She was silent.

He added, "Please."

I can't let myself get carried away by how happy I am to see him again. I can't! She used humor as her defense. "You bet your ass you have a lot to tell me."

He laughed at her saucy, sarcastic tone and pose. "You've added some new stuff to your act, I see."

"There's one thing I have to know up front, Saunders. Before you disappeared I saw a family with you. Who are they? Are they your family? I saw rings on your fingers. Why didn't you tell me about them?" She wanted to be the sassy creature audiences went crazy for on stage, but there was no way to keep the accusation and hurt out of her voice.

She needed those answers before he disappeared again.

"I didn't know about it to share with you. Now, I remember. Now, I can tell you. Please give me a chance to explain. I didn't know you could see them. When I looked back you were gone."

"So, tell me." Hands on her sides, she stared him in the eyes.

"Here?" Saunders gestured to the creatures floating close by. "I've never lied to you. I swear it."

Sighing with obvious impatience, she swam fast to the side entrance of her room in Riddle's sandcastle. "I already forgave you and let go, but we've been friends so come in and say what you want to say."

He settled into the large, pillow-soft chair opposite the lilac-colored loveseat Velvet sat on.

She blinked, the only movement she made while she sat holding his stare.

"Okay." He laughed. "What you saw was my brain recreating a scene I read in a novel close to when I had my accident. I went fishing, hit my head, and was pulled here. That's what I think happened."

She doubted it could be so simple, but then again, she knew where they were. What he was saying could be true.

"That has been my least favorite part of the Dreaming," he continued. "Not being able to control when we were separated. I wonder why you were able to see that vision."

Velvet was still trying to stifle her feelings, waiting for more reasons to believe that she wasn't going to be hurt again.

"Did you see the cabin, Velvet? It seems like I've been trying to get back to it forever. I was finally able to go inside. That's when I found most of what I needed to know and remembered the rest."

She couldn't miss the nervous way he twisted his fingers together or the earnest expression in his eyes as he tried to explain. She gave him a small break. "What did you need to know?"

"That I've been given a choice, like the message said. Only, I needed to know what my options were."

"Maybe my choosing not to see you anymore helped you find your answers." The mystery was more intriguing than holding onto her guard or reminding him of her pain.

"You know I never wanted to hurt you. And you did choose to see me. That's why we're here, now."

Velvet shook her head, and this time, she softened her tone. "I didn't have a choice. You were surrounding me."

"Oh." His shoulders slumped. "What I feel for you is why I'm here. I didn't think about what would happen if you didn't want to be with me. I chose to give up my life to be with you."

That registered with her. Velvet leaned forward, staring into his earnest eyes. "You have to die in your world to be with me?"

"No, Velvet, staying in my world would be the real death. By choosing to stay with you, I'm living for the first time. I want the life I only read about before from great poets. You're everything to me."

"You mean it." This was her Saunders. He was different now that he had his memories back. There was a new confidence in the way he spoke. The way he moved. She went to him, certain that he knew exactly who he was, and what he wanted.

"Oh, Saunders." She sighed through happy tears and messy kisses. "Do you feel that? I feel different. Do you?"

"I do. This is where I was meant to be. I've finally found my home." He wrapped his arms around her.

Chapter 13

"WOW." SAUNDERS WIGGLED his fingers. "I feel all kinds of energized. Like I drank a triple espresso."

"That's good, right?" Velvet shifted her weight on his lap, her lavender fin firm on his thighs. She looked into his eyes.

"It's fantastic! Is this how you feel?" The smile on her face was a clear yes.

"I do now because I know you're here to stay."

Sex is going to be intense. Wait, is sex even possible? Was it too soon to ask her about it? There was more than sex to think about. At least, that's what he told his libido.

He stroked her creamy skin. She was petite enough to wrap his hands around her waist. The electric sizzle he felt when they touched before he made his choice was stronger now. "Does this feel different?"

The little gasp she made when he brushed against her hip told him the answer.

There was a knock at the door.

"That will be Riddle. He probably felt it when you-" She wiggled her fingers, then moved off his lap to open the door.

"Died. It's okay to say it, Velvet. There are no regrets."

Velvet opened the door to welcome Riddle.

Saunders tried not to stare when Riddle hop-skipped into the room.

"Riddle, this is Saunders. Saunders, Riddle is the friend who gave us the clue."

"This isn't heaven. Humans don't die in the World to come live here for eternity. When I saw how much you and Velvet cared for each other I found a way to bring you here. It only worked because it was what you wanted, too." Riddle nodded at them and then hop-skipped back through the door, closing it behind him.

"He didn't let me thank him." Saunders said. "Are we supposed to follow him?"

She shook her head. "He's shy. He rarely speaks to anyone. It's amazing that Riddle did this for us. It all makes sense now. It took his power to make it happen."

"We should find a way to thank him that won't embarrass him," Saunders said. She beamed a different smile at him. "I can tell what you're feeling by how you smile now. This one is about your friend." He traced her lips with his fingertips.

That earned him a quick kiss. "A simple nod will be enough for him. He's happy. I can feel it."

"A nod. Got it. Now what do we do about me being homeless? I was before, when I was a teenager. I'm not worried, more like curious."

"Homeless?" She quirked her head to the side.

"I have no home here."

"The whole Dreaming is your home."

"I'm used to where there are lots of rules. Are you saying I can go wherever I want and build a house? Are houses already made that I can pick from?"

"You can make a house wherever you want."

Saunders focused on her room for the first time. There was no bed because she didn't sleep. No kitchen because she didn't eat. No bathroom. The only furniture was the couch they were sitting on. One wall was filled with pictures; of the sandcastle, the mermaid he'd seen her with when they'd finally reconnected, one of her and Riddle. The largest two were in the center, side by side. One was of him, and the other was the two of them during their first kiss. Wait, it wasn't a picture. It was a video that played when he focused on it.

"I'd like to have one of these in my house." He motioned to the video.

"Done. There's a copy waiting. It will be there when you decide where you want your house to be and what you want it to look like."

"Do I get to do that, too? Or do I have to take a class? Pass a test?"

Velvet shook her head. "You imagine what you want and where you want it. Then it appears."

Saunders whistled. He held out a hand, inviting her to go with him.

"This is exciting!" Her tail fluttered.

"Let's see what you think of this." Saunders followed her instructions, forming his dream home. He chose the façade of an old colonial he owned. No, used to own.

His will would provide funding and instructions to include the colonial mansion in the Saunders O'Brien Youth Foundation. His first name meant gypsy. He'd never thought of himself as one, but looking back now, he saw that he had tendencies. Like following the urge to update his will before he took off on his extended leave to the cabin. *I knew I wasn't going back.*

He set his mind to the simple structure he wanted to create. Three rooms. The largest would be filled with stars, because Velvet loved them. Another was built around a sapphire blue swimming pool because he loved to swim. The final room was a movie theater. They hadn't talked about it much, but he loved TV and movies as much as she did.

"Ready?" He was taking a risk in *where* he placed his home. His sole intention was for the Dreaming to choose the best place for it based on what it knew about him and Velvet.

They instinctively closed their eyes and waited, energy swirling around them.

"It's done," Velvet whispered.

"Should we look on the count of three?" Saunders asked.

"Yes. You count." She wiggled as they stood together, holding hands.

"One, two, three!"

They hadn't moved. They stood in the star-filled room he'd imagined where stars twinkled and floated in the air. There was a doorway to the right where he could see the pool he designed. A curving iron scrollwork stairway led to a balcony. He knew the movie theater was up there.

"Huh?" He said.

Velvet was speechless.

"I wasn't trying to change your room. Or impose on you. I asked the Dreaming to put me where it thought it would be best for you and me."

"My pictures and my couch are still here, and they're all I care about. The Dreaming isn't wrong. Riddle must have agreed, too. Nothing overrides his magic."

"I'm glad to hear it if this means he's okay with me moving in here. How about you? You want to live with me?" He wanted her to say yes. He wanted to share everything with her.

"Is it weird that I never thought about us living apart?"

"No." Saunders scooped her up in his arms. She was weightless. The current he'd been wishing would show up and move her long, silky hair obliged, showing lilac nipples. Man, she was sexy. Her skin was soft and dewy like rose petals. He leaned in and nudged her lips with his, his tongue slipping into her open, waiting mouth.

He was harder than he'd ever been, but he wouldn't rush. There was too much he didn't know. "You taste like strawberries and cream."

"I've heard that's a compliment." Velvet smiled. She ran her hand down his arm, feeling the muscles in his biceps.

"Can you?" He pressed his hard on against her thigh.

"Have sex?" Her eyes were on his shorts.

The way she said it was pure sensation. He hoped with all his being that they could.

"Yes. I've done it before."

He was conflicted about what he did and didn't want to know about past lovers. All he cared about was their love and letting her take the lead.

"You'll know when I'm ready," she said, kissing his jaw.

If she wasn't going to hesitate, he wasn't either. He ran his hands down her bare back, enjoying the way she shivered and whimpered in his ear.

Velvet ran her hands down his chest, grasped his waistband, and pushed his shorts off.

He lowered his head to take her hardened nipple into his mouth, sucking until she moaned and threw her head back.

"I need to tell you what I didn't tell you before, when I said I've done it. What I meant is, I've done it with creatures but never with a human like you. I've made out, but it stopped before the..."

"Before the part where it goes inside? I don't know what I'm doing here, baby. I just know that I want to love you."

"I want that, too. I'm almost ready. Will you go slow?"

Her husky voice was driving him crazy. "Yes."

Velvet took his cock in her hand and rubbed her finger across the top of his head.

His hips jerked when she closed her fist around him.

"Here." Velvet guided his hand to her curvy hips. "Pet me."

Her hips were sizzling hot. Finding out what would happen if he kissed her there became an obsession. He licked and kissed just below her waist, between her hips. The scales thinned, creating an opening.

"Come here." Velvet said, leading him to the couch. "Ride me, like this."

He straddled her hips the way she asked him to and let her ease his hard dick inside. It was fiery, welcoming heat. Almost too tight to move. The pleasure was mind blowing. He had to distract himself so he would last long enough for her.

She gripped his hips, pushing and pulling slowly, then faster as she panted and grabbed him for a kiss.

He broke their kiss long enough to tell her she was incredible before he met her urgent kisses with his own. She was slick yet tighter than before.

"Faster now," she said.

If this wasn't it, he was going to enjoy making it up to her. He let go, driving into her, locking his eyes on hers to share the moment when their passion peaked.

Juice squirted from her, coating him in insane sensation that pulled an explosive orgasm out of him.

She was groaning and reaching for him, urging him to keep going.

"You want more?" He knew she did. It turned him on more to say the words. He wasn't going to pull out. No force in any world could stop him from giving her another orgasm. The way her body squeezed him was intoxicating. He thought they would go slow and savor it this time. Her fevered cries demanded that he speed up and give her all he could until they came together, each one driving the other crazy with lust.

They started again, sharing orgasm after orgasm, until a bell rang.

"What's that?" Saunders stopped to ask, trying to make sense of the noise.

She cupped his bare ass, urging him closer to her tail. "I don't want to stop. In fact, I won't." The bell rang again. She sighed. "It's my manager, Cassidy. We were planning for her to come over to talk about a new tour."

"You mean I have to share you?" He teased, easing away from her. She looked like they'd spent all their time making love with her tousled hair and sated smile.

"No, but I want you to meet her. She's one of my favorite creatures to spend time with."

In the time it would take him to blink if he still needed to, Velvet's hair was back in place. Her smile stayed sexy. He liked it.

Velvet made quick introductions and plans to meet another time, explaining that she wanted to talk to Saunders about the tour. Cassidy agreed and left with a parting compliment about how she liked the new room.

"You didn't have to make her leave for me. I know what it's like to work for what you want. It takes time and commitment. But since you did, thank you." Saunders bowed and moved closer to where she stood by the door.

"I know I didn't have to and that you're not going to disappear, but I still feel an urgency to be alone with you. Here." Velvet clasped her hands over her heart.

"I wonder what I did to deserve you. To deserve this." Saunders motioned to the rooms around them.

"Amazing is what the Dreaming does best." Velvet smiled. "I think the Dreaming showed you to me because it knew I would help you. My interest in the World isn't normal. Most creatures don't know it exists."

"Is the Dreaming about fulfilling wishes? What I was doing when I took a break from my work was what humans call *finding yourself*. It took everything I had to get back to you. Being here with you is what I wanted, but I didn't know you were possible. Maybe the Dreaming is about granting miracles."

"You could be right. There's a story in the Hall of Records about The Dreaming being created because of a miracle."

"We'll visit there, won't we? I know it's one of your favorite places."

Velvet nodded.

He held out a hand to guide her upstairs into the theater. "I want to show you what it's like to sit at the back of a movie theater on a date."

Saunders settled them in black plush seats like he'd designed for his own mansion. He practiced intention by putting a romantic comedy on the screen to set the mood.

"You know what I like." Velvet squeezed his hand.

He stared into her luminous eyes. "Is there more of the Dreaming that you haven't seen? I'd love to explore it with you."

"I've always wanted to be with someone who wanted to explore with me."

Saunders leaned in for a kiss that ended in a laugh when the couple on the screen closed the curtains.

The End was spelled out on the curtains in white light.

About The Author

GINA BRIGANTI WRITES fantasy and sci-fi romance in north Texas. She also writes holistic health non-fiction because real life can be magic, too. Her credentials in holistic health include certification as a Reiki Master Practitioner and teacher, certification as a nutrition consultant, and a degree in holistic nutrition.

When she's not writing, eating delicious healthy food, reading, or making videos, she is spending time with family and friends. Her constant companion is a special soul who masquerades as a lab and chow mix.

Connect with Gina:

Join the newsletter community now[1] to get Owl Vs. Animal Charmers as a thank you gift. This story features Lucy and Stan from Desert Sunrise (Book 2).

<u>Facebook Author Page</u>[2]

<u>Blog</u>[3]

<u>Goodreads</u>[4]

<u>Instagram</u>[5]

<u>Twitter</u>[6]

<u>Bookbub</u>[7]

---

1. https://ginabriganti.us8.list-manage.com/sub-scribe?u=efb8eaf5e244c4ac83bb036d2&id=2bb9bdfd73

2. https://www.facebook.com/ginabrigantiauthor/?modal=admin_todo_tour

3. http://www.ginabriganti.com

4. https://www.goodreads.com/author/show/4236998.Gina_Briganti

5. https://www.instagram.com/ginabriganti/

6. https://twitter.com/brigantigina

7. https://www.bookbub.com/profile/gina-briganti

The Dreaming
Natural Gifts Book 1

Dreams and psychic connections become reality in this fantasy romance.

SINGLE MOM DANA CARAPELLI wakes up in a parallel world called the Dreaming for the first time the night before she meets a handsome rancher. When she wakes up in the Dreaming again she is on his ranch. He knows all about the Dreaming because he wakes up there every time he falls asleep. He admits that he has been promised a perfect partner for him and his teenage son but doesn't know if it's her. Family and friends caution her to take it slow and that's without telling them what she knows will make them sound crazy. Joe is everything her dead husband wasn't. What if it's her turn to be happy?

What if it's real?

Start the journey into this fantasy romance today[1]!

---

1.   https://www.amazon.com/Dreaming-Natural-Gifts-Book-ebook/dp/ B00IV1NEC6/

Desert Sunrise
Natural Gifts Book 2

A hot one night stand after her best friend's wedding could not turn into her wildest fantasy come true. Could it? Their best friends haven't been hiding a connection to a parallel world or the fact that they're sharing a psychic bond that will change everything they know is true and real. Right?

RESTAURANT CRITIC LUCY Shannon's ex-fiancé put her heart in a blender and punched the puree button. A couple years of therapy later she knows how to enjoy herself for a night when the right ranch foreman asks.

Stan Spellman has seen one or two happily married couples but his heart has never been stolen. Lucy's a safe bet since she lives hours away from Sunny Skies Stables.

They'll find out what they unlocked the moment they were introduced; a soul mate bond and their own set of extraordinary gifts.

The bond will bring them together however it has to.

BUY DESERT SUNRISE today[1] and immerse yourself in this twisty, sexy fantasy romance.

No Yesterdays
Natural Gifts Book 3

Soul mates are being drawn together in numbers we've never seen. Gifts are unlocking faster than racing hearts, adding eight new people to the soul group. The group is growing, their energy blending in ways they didn't know could happen. The big question is why is the soul mate bond in a hurry?

BRITTANY HAS BEEN PINING for Carter for years now. She needs a push.

Jack is stubborn personified and close to having Darah walk away, keeping her secrets to herself. They need a shove.

Jason is having the time of his life in college. All those beautiful women. Ha. Not the plan. Angelina can handle him.

Rowan is convinced that his soul mate didn't incarnate with him in this lifetime. Surprise! This psychic finds out exactly why the women in his family told him his arrogance was blinding.

There's no looking back now.

There are No Yesterdays.

BUY NO YESTERDAYS[1] to join in on the fantasy and the romance today.

1. *https://www.amazon.com/No-Yesterdays-Natural-Gifts-Book-ebook/dp/B079CQPVD8/*

Deep In The Dreaming
Natural Gifts Book 4

A parallel world. A trapped soul. To save her friends, they'll battle addiction, magic, and eternity...

ELENA ZUCCHERO HAS lived and lost in reality. Now she fills her heart through her work as a hypnotherapist by helping her patients improve their lives. But when a nightmare plagues her sleep, she learns her friends have gone missing in an addictive alternate plane. And the only way to save them may require feeding the demons of her handsome new client...

Draper Montgomery painfully resists the call of the Dreaming. But despite his dangerous cravings, he senses his enchanting therapist has a wound he can help heal. And to satisfy his heart's desire, he may just have to risk the very foundation of his mind...

As Elena and Draper discover a deeper soul connection, the therapist struggles to keep her distance in the hunt for her friends. If the people she loves even want to be saved...

Will the perilous hunt to rescue her friends lose them their lives and their souls?

Deep in the Dreaming is the fourth book in the captivating Natural Gifts fantasy romance series. If you like mysterious worlds, conflicted characters, and love that conquers all, then you'll adore Gina Briganti's enthralling tale.

Buy Deep in the Dreaming [1] to slip into another world today!

1.   https://www.amazon.com/Deep-Dreaming-Natural-Gifts-Book-ebook/dp/
      B07PQTPHF3/

Don't miss out!

Visit the website below and you can sign up to receive emails whenever Gina Briganti publishes a new book. There's no charge and no obligation.

https://books2read.com/r/B-A-ALYH-YXSDB

BOOKS 2 READ

Connecting independent readers to independent writers.

Made in the USA
Coppell, TX
05 March 2020

16534925R00055